Dinosaurs Don't Bark

Written & Illustrated by Amir Mortel
Published by Funky Dreamer Storytime

Dinosaurs Don't Bark

ISBN-13: 978-1790453504
Published by **Funky Dreamer Storytime**

Funky Dreamer Storytime
Greg Wachs
www.funkydreamerstorytime.com
310-966-7536
greg@funkydreamerstorytime.com
mediacom2020@gmail.com
Twitter: @podcasts4kids

Amir Mortel can be reached via Upwork.com or at
amircmortel@gmail.com

Ordering Information

Special discounts are available on quantity purchases
by corporations, education, K12, and associations. For
details, contact the publisher at the info above. Orders
by bookstores and wholesalers, please contact us at
the info above.

Listen to **Funky Dreamer Podcasts4Kids** on **iTunes**
or at **www.funkydreamerstorytime.com**

Dedication

To my prayer partner, dance partner, and forever girlfriend,
Hazel, this is it!

To our little boy, bundle of joy, Adam,
may you appreciate books first before gadgets.

– Amir Mortel

"Later Mom."

Adam refused to have carrot sticks for a snack. He was busy playing a game on his tablet.

"It's a long drive Adam, you need to eat something on our way there," his dad said.

"Later Dad," Adam said, his eyes glued to the tablet.

A familiar tune came on the radio,
as his dad started singing along.

"C'mon honey, join us!" his mom said.
Adam stared at the screen, silent.

Finally, they arrived at the beach.
Adam's dad got the grill ready,
while his mom set up the tent.

Spotty was off sniffing around,
but Adam just sat on a beach chair,
staring at his tablet.

[Beep-beep-beep]

"Mooom? Can I please have the battery pack?" Adam yelled.

Nothing.

"I guess they're busy," Adam thought.

"Ruff! Ruff!" Spotty ran up with a twig, wanting to play fetch.

"Later Spotty," Adam mumbled, without even looking up.

Spotty walked away sad.

"Where is everybody?"
Adam asked.

Adam popped his head
inside the tent, then
popped back out.

"What the...?" He muttered.

Down on the ground were HUGE footprints.

"Huh? Wow, there must be REALLY BIG chickens around here!" he thought nervously, crawling into the tent.

THUD! THUD!
The ground trembled.

Adam held his breath
and listened.

THUD! THUD!
The sound grew louder.

A shadow passed
over the tent.

Adam heard a growl.

He was scared, but curious. He peeked his head through the tent flap and looked around.

Nothing.

He slipped out, and tiptoed around to the back of the tent.

GULP! He was suddenly face-to-face with a huge, brown-colored, scaly giant staring back at him.

"Grrr…" the dinosaur growled softly.

"Waaaaahhhhh!" Adam screamed
and ran for his life.

The dinosaur chased him, growling, close behind.

"Ruff Ruff!" it barked. "Wait, did that dino just bark?" or was that Spotty? Adam asked.

Adam spotted a narrow cave and
ducked just in time!

The angry dino stopped and growled,
too big to fit in.

Once inside the cave, Adam noticed drawings on the wall.

Then he saw it! A caveman and cavewoman sitting around a campfire.

"Maybe they can help me," Adam thought.

They looked surprisingly familiar to him.

"Uh, Mom?... Dad?" he asked.

"Ooga-ooga!" said the cavewoman
dressed in animal fur, and glaring at him.

"Ooga-Ooga!!!" the full-bearded caveman shouted,
raising his club, and stomping towards him.

Angry cavepeople inside, growling dinosaur outside.
Adam was trapped, consumed with fear, head down, shaking.

Then, trembling and sweaty, his head began spinning.
His vision dimmed, and then... just black.

"Wait, what's this?" Adam thought.
"It's licking my face?
But who? Caveman? Dinosaur?"

Adam heard a growl.

"Ahhhh, the dino is licking my face!"
His face was dripping wet!

Adam decided to open his eyes.

"Spotty!" he shouted. Adam was so happy he couldn't help but hug Spotty.

"So it was a dream! Thank God! I thought I was going to be dino-food," Adam sighed.

"Are you alright?" his mom yelled, rushing to see what had happened.

"Yes Mom, we were just playing," he replied.

"Here's the battery pack Honey, you dropped it inside the car," his mom said.

Adam paused for a couple of seconds.

"Uh, no thanks Mom, Spotty and I are gonna play." he replied.

"Hey guys, it's time to eat!" Adam's dad called.

Adam quickly put down the tablet and sat on the picnic blanket.

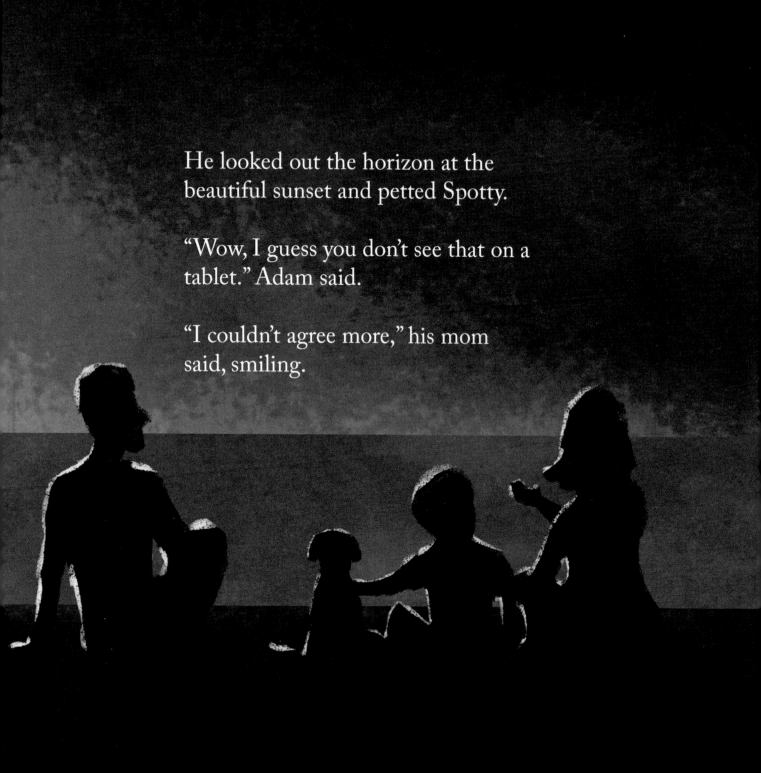

He looked out the horizon at the beautiful sunset and petted Spotty.

"Wow, I guess you don't see that on a tablet." Adam said.

"I couldn't agree more," his mom said, smiling.

Funky Dreamer Storytime creates unique books for kids and publishes up and coming new kids authors! We are excited to support Amir Mortel as both author and illustrator!

About the Author

Amir Mortel is a Graphic Designer, Book Wizard, a loving husband to his wife Hazel, and a doting father to an 18-month toddler, Adam.

He loves eating carrot sticks, sings along with tunes on the radio, barbecueing, and playing tag with dinosaurs XD.

Remember kids, some of these books are podbooks,
which means they have a matching podcast!

Just go to www.funkydreamerstorytime.com
or search **iTunes** for the name of the book.

Each podcast reads you the book.
They are also chock full of really cool music!

**So, fire up a podcast, kick back
and enjoy the adventure!**

Enjoy All The Books From Funky Dreamer Storytime.

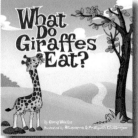    

Made in the USA
Coppell, TX
14 December 2019